Can one balloon make an elephant fly?

by Dan Richards and
Jeff Newman

SIMON & SCHUSTER BOOKS FOR YOUNG READERS
NEW YORK LONDON TORONTO SYDNEY NEW DELHI

For you, Evan, two balloons should be plenty to make a hippopotamus fly.

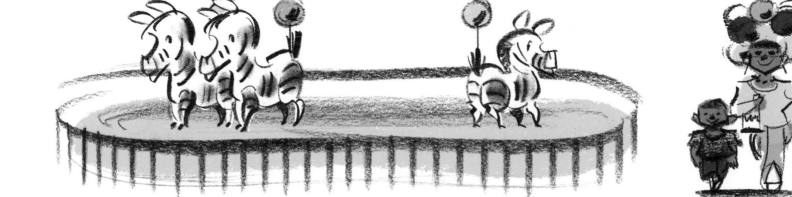

To Kelly, my little red balloon
—D. R.

To Mom
—J. N.

SIMON & SCHUSTER BOOKS FOR YOUNG READERS
An imprint of Simon & Schuster Children's Publishing Division • 1230
Avenue of the Americas, New York, New York 10020 • Text copyright ©
2016 by Dan Richards • Illustrations copyright © 2016 by Jeff Newman •
All rights reserved, including the right of reproduction in whole or in part
in any form. • SIMON & SCHUSTER BOOKS FOR YOUNG READERS is
a trademark of Simon & Schuster, Inc. • For information about special
discounts for bulk purchases, please contact Simon & Schuster Special
Sales at 1-866-506-1949 or business@simonandschuster.com. • The Simon
& Schuster Speakers Bureau can bring authors to your live event. For
more information or to book an event, contact the Simon & Schuster Speakers
Bureau at 1-866-248-3049 or visit our website at www.simonspeakers.com. •
Book design by Alicia Mikles • The text for this book is set in Geometric
Slabserif 70. • The illustrations for this book were rendered using charcoal
and crayon, then digitally composited. • Manufactured in China •
0616 SCP • First Edition • 10 9 8 7 6 5 4 3 2 1 • Library of
Congress Cataloging-in-Publication Data • Names: Richards, Dan, 1966–
| Newman, Jeff, 1976– ill. • Title: Can one balloon make an elephant fly? /
Dan Richards ; with pictures by Jeff Newman. • Description: | Summary:
A mother takes her son to the zoo to answer his science question. •
Identifiers: LCCN 2012013297 | ISBN 9781442452152 (hardcover) —
ISBN 9781442452176 (eBook) • Subjects: | CYAC: Mother and child—
Fiction. | Zoo animals—Fiction. | Balloons—Fiction. | Flight—Fiction. •
Classification: LCC PZ7.R3788 Can 2016 | DDC [E]—dc23 LC record
available at http://lccn.loc.gov/2012013297